J PB
Amarel, Connie.
How does the dragonfly?
c2015

How Does the Dragonfly?

Written by Connie Amarel
Illustrated by Swapan Debnath

ISBN 978-1-61225-313-8

Published by Mirror Publishing
Milwaukee, WI 53214

Printed in the USA.

This book is dedicated to children everywhere, young and old, who are fascinated by the magical abilities of dragonflies. It is also dedicated with love and admiration to my wonderful friends, Anjali and Ranjana, who inspired and encouraged me to write this story. A most special thank you to the amazing children at my Wednesday story time at the Village Library: Kiali, Ciara, Maria, River, Jacob, Violet, Ezra, and Diana. Your interest and enthusiasm encouraged me to have this story published. Many thanks go to my wonderful publisher Neal and my unbelievably talented illustrator Swapan. This book is especially dedicated with love and appreciation to my incredible family for their endless love and support.

RJ worked in her lab deep into the night, putting the finishing touches on her prized invention, a beautiful robotic dragonfly. RJ was captivated by the magical flying ability of dragonflies.

Her robotic dragonfly had magnificent detail, but as hard as RJ tried, she couldn't duplicate the amazing and highly skilled flying ability that a dragonfly possesses.

So RJ programmed her robotic dragonfly, which she named Angie, to mingle with real dragonflies. She hoped to gain valuable insight into what gives dragonflies their magical flying abilities.

RJ took Angie to a pond out in a meadow where she had seen so many dragonflies in the past. She kissed Angie and told her to learn all the information she could about dragonflies.

RJ watched Angie circle the pond several times and then fly out over the meadow. She watched as Angie flew away, joining a group of dragonflies who were flying at the far end of the meadow.

As Angie flew out of sight, RJ crossed her fingers that the real dragonflies would accept a robotic dragonfly into their group and also share valuable information with her.

Angie flew alongside the real dragonflies and asked where they were going. One of the dragonflies, named Clara, told Angie they were going to school. Angie asked if she could join them and Clara said, "Yes!"

Clara noticed that Angie looked different than the other dragonflies. Angie explained that she was a robotic dragonfly and she was hoping to learn valuable information about dragonflies so she could be more like them.

When they arrived at school, Clara introduced Angie to Mr. Cook, the teacher. He was so excited to meet a robotic dragonfly. Mr. Cook had often dreamed about the possibility that someday there would be a robotic dragonfly and now he realized that his dream had come true.

Mr. Cook introduced Angie to the rest of the class and set up a desk for her to sit at. He then began his lecture starting with the history of the dragonfly. Angie listened intently, recording every word that he spoke.

He told the class that dragonflies were some of the first winged insects, evolving 300 million years ago. He said that modern dragonflies have wingspans of two to five inches, but that fossils of dragonflies have been found having wingspans of up to two feet. This made the class gasp.

The students learned that the reason dragonflies grew to such monstrous size may have been due to the high oxygen levels during the Paleozoic Era. Mr. Clark also told the class that dragonflies belong to the Odonata order, which means "toothed one" in Greek and that this referred to the dragonfly's serrated teeth.

1 foot

6 inches

Angie was amazed at the fascinating history of dragonflies. She listened closely to every word that Mr. Cook said. Angie knew that RJ would be amazed by this fascinating history as well.

Mr. Cook explained why dragonflies have excellent vision. He told the class that the head of a dragonfly consists almost entirely of two huge compound eyes, giving dragonflies nearly 360° vision. They can see a wider spectrum of color than humans and their remarkable vision helps them detect the movement of other insects and avoid collisions.

Angie raised her hand and asked Mr. Cook, "How does a dragonfly?" Mr. Cook responded, "I think you're asking, 'How does a dragonfly fly?'" Hearing Mr. Cook say this made the students burst into laughter. When they had gotten quiet again, Mr. Cook said, "Actually, Angie, that is a great question."

He told the class that a bee flaps its wings about 300 times per second, but a dragonfly flaps its wings about 30 beats per second. This is due to dragonflies having two sets of larger wings so they don't have to beat them as much to fly. The students gave each other a high-five after hearing this. Clara smiled at Angie and gave her a high-five.

1 foot

6 inches

Mr. Cook continued that dragonflies are very strong and good fliers and can fly up to speeds of 30 miles per hour, moving each of their four wings independently. In addition to flapping their wings up and down, they can rotate their wings back and forth, enabling them to put on an aerial show like no other.

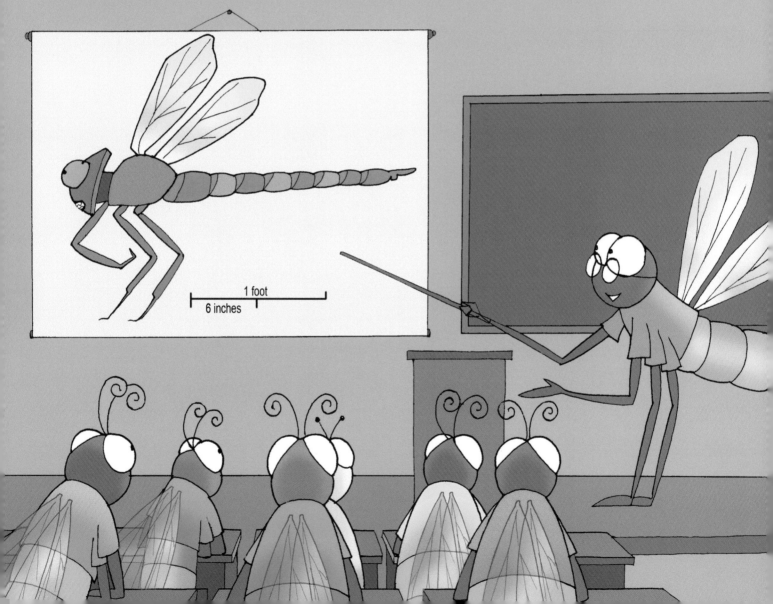

He said that dragonflies can move straight up and down, stop and hover like a helicopter, and make hairpin turns at full speed or in slow motion. They even mate in mid-air. He stated that if dragonflies can't fly they'll starve because they only eat prey they catch while flying.

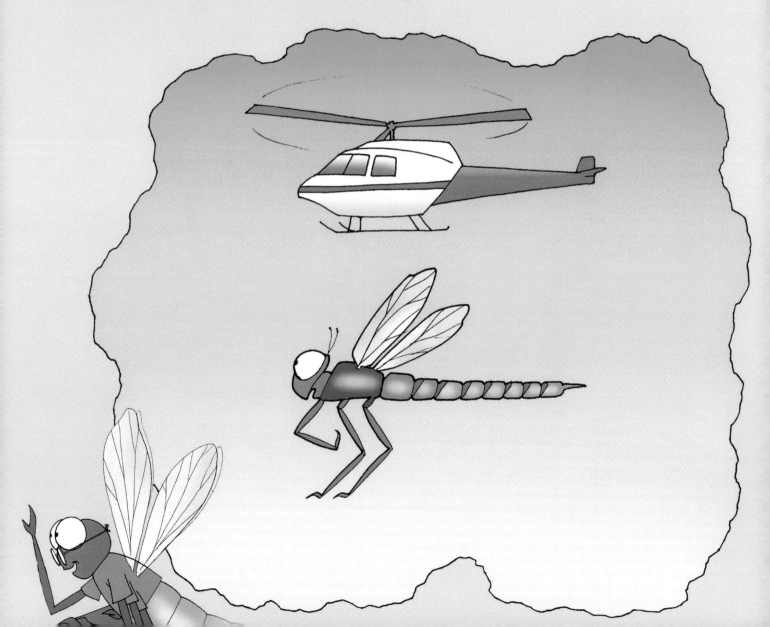

Angie looked at the other students with awe and admiration. She was so impressed at the incredible amount of talent and ability each of them possessed. Just then Mr. Cook announced that class was over for the day and that he hoped they would have a wonderful weekend.

Clara asked Angie if she would like to come home with her, but Angie explained that she needed to get back to the lab to share all the wonderful information she had learned with RJ. Angie asked Clara if she would like to come to the lab with her and meet RJ. Clara happily said, "Yes!"

The other students came over to say goodbye to Angie and that they looked forward to seeing her in class on Monday. Then in unison they asked, "Hey Angie, how does the dragonfly?" Angie laughed and told them, "With help from my friends!"

RJ was anxiously waiting when Angie and Clara arrived at the lab. Angie introduced her new friend to RJ and told her about joining the other students in class. Angie said that the teacher, Mr. Cook, was very knowledgeable and that she learned so much from him.

Just then all the wonderful and valuable information came spilling out. RJ listened with pride as Angie told her about everything she had learned. She was especially happy that Angie had been accepted by the real dragonflies, even though she was a robotic dragonfly.

When Angie and Clara went out to the meadow to practice flying maneuvers, RJ clapped her hands with joy. She realized that her invention had become even more special than she could ever have imagined.

CPSIA information can be obtained at www.ICGtesting.com
Printed in the USA
LVIW01n1754170915
454366LV00008B/33